W9-BCS-576

STORY AND PICTURES BY

THE SNOW FOX

A TALE OF CANADA

ARNOLD DOBRIN

COWARD-MC CANN INC. • NEW YORK

 Library of Congress Catalog Card Number: 68-23864 Printed in the United States of America

Outside in the evening twilight the dogs barked excitedly.

Peter heard the tinkling of faint sleighbells in the distance and knew that his father was coming home. "He's back! He's back!" he shouted. Rushing to the front door, he flung it open and waded out into the deep snow.

His mother followed, hugging a sweater around herself tightly, smoothing her hair, and smiling with delight. The air was icy and tingling. Partly to keep warm, partly from excitement, Peter flung his arms around and jumped up and down.

The sound of the sleighbells grew nearer, and in a moment the sleigh turned the bend in the road and came into sight. The evening air rang with shouts of "Welcome home!" Peter felt himself being lifted high in the air and the roughness of his father's beard against his face. He kissed him and laughed when his father whirled him around in the freezing dark evening.

Then his father called out, "Enough, enough! Only animals stay out in the Canadian winter! Let's go in the house."

While Peter's mother set the table for dinner, his father unloaded the big mounds of heavy pelts from the sled, for Peter's father was a fur trapper.

Peter warmed himself in front of the fire, keeping his eyes on the back door. He could hardly wait to hear about all the exciting things that had happened while his father had been away. When his father finally came in, he carried a bag with something round and soft-looking in the bottom. It seemed to be moving.

Peter ran into the kitchen.

Settling wearily into a chair, his father said, "I was lucky this trip. I got an Arctic fox—the snow fox—one of the most valuable furs there are. Inside"—he shook his head in the direction of the shed—"is the most beautiful fox skin I've ever seen—from a vixen, a female."

Then he turned to Peter. "After I killed her, I stumbled across her lair and found her pups, but they all ran away as quickly as they could—except this little fellow. How would you like to take care of him?"

Peter was too excited to speak. He knelt down beside the bag.

The little fox lifted his nose, scenting him. Peter reached out his hand and laid it gently on the soft neck. Then he carefully picked up the small creature, cradling it in his arms. How soft and fine was the delicate fur! It looked as white as the snow and smelled of the pine trees and wild grasses. "Niki is your name," Peter said.

At first he was afraid the fox would snap at him. The animal quivered as Peter held him, but when he turned his large wild eyes to look at the boy, Peter knew he loved the little creature more than any pet he had ever had.

Peter's mother called, "Supper's ready." They all were so hungry that they ate silently, enjoying the warmth and flavor of the food. Then the family moved to chairs in front of the fire.

They were just comfortably settled when Peter's mother spoke. "Now that you have eaten," she said in a weary voice, "I have some bad news for you."

With a worried look, Peter's father asked, "What is it?"

"During the night we heard nothing at all," said his mother, "but when I went out to milk this morning, I found one of the calves killed. The prints in the snow weren't clear, but I could see that one paw had only three toes."

"Ah!" Peter's father slammed his fist down on the table angrily. He hated Three-Toes—the wolf that had raided the neighborhood since the beginning of autumn. Three-Toes was not an ordinary wolf, who killed for food when he was hungry. Three-Toes—who had lost the other toes in a fight or a trap—was a killer wolf, who killed only for the sake of the kill.

As they talked, the fire roared and crackled merrily. Peter listened to his parents and watched the glowing embers. He imagined that two of the brightly glowing coals were the eyes of the killer wolf staring at him. "Why would an animal kill," Peter asked aloud, "when he isn't even hungry?"

"No one knows, Peter," his father answered. "It's one of nature's mysteries. Killing is natural for most animals. They must kill to live. As for the others—well, we must see to it that they are stopped from senseless killing."

Peter's father had talked about nature before. It was mysterious, but little by little, Peter was learning more about it. Every day he discovered something in the great forests that surrounded their village. He loved to go deep into the forest's lonely places, to watch the animals living their busy lives.

Last summer he had built a tree house. It was his secret place where he took only best friends. Someday when Niki was grown, he would show it to him.

The snow fox grew quickly. His fur became thicker and whiter. He was a very clever animal and learned to come when his name was called. Throughout the day he was usually at Peter's side. At night he slept on the porch in a box that Peter had made for him.

The first time Peter took Niki to the village nearby, everyone stopped to look at the snow fox. "A fox for a pet!" an old man exclaimed. "You are a little fool, Peter. Do you think you can make a real pet out of a fox?"

Soon everyone in the village grew used to the idea that Peter had a fox for a pet. Still, most of the villagers waited for the day when he would show his wild nature. Even the children would say, "You think he is a fox, Peter, but someday he will outfox you!"

Peter didn't want to believe what he heard. He wasn't sure what he believed, but he knew that somehow, whatever happened, Niki would always be his friend.

"Come on, Niki," he said to the fox as he got up, "I want to show you my own house in the forest."

Together they started down the path that led behind the houses of the village. In the soft pale light of the wintry sun, the white snow was bright and dazzling. Huge sparkling icicles hung from the rooftops of the houses, and the snow creaked and scrunched under Peter's feet.

The sounds of the village quickly faded. The great forest was silent. After a short time, he crouched in the snow and said, "Look, Niki"—he pointed to a line of faint animal tracks—"Do you know what kind of animal made these?"

Niki sniffed without much interest.

Then Peter said, "A rabbit made those tracks," for he was proud of being able to tell the tracks of the animals.

But as his eyes followed the rabbit tracks, he frowned. After a few yards the tracks were stopped by another pair of tracks. The snow was disturbed, and the rabbit tracks did not continue. Peter shivered.

Together they went on, Niki trotting at Peter's side or darting from tree to tree to investigate the smell of a furrow or a fallen log. Except for the bobbing point of his small black nose, he faded into the white world of the forest so completely that Peter could barely see him.

Before long they came to a huge tree. "We're here," Peter said as he began to climb. The tree house was not very high, and the big thick branches made it easy for Niki to follow. From the tree house Peter saw that the daylight was almost gone. How quickly it got dark in winter! Already a pale crescent of moon was riding the cold blue evening sky.

Peter pulled his scarf more tightly around his neck and said, "This is our house, and only you and I can come here whenever we want. Oh, maybe once in a while we will ask a friend, but it really belongs only to us. And look at this..."

Peter pointed to part of an old desk, the kind that has many tiny drawers. He pulled open one that was stuffed with acorns. Another had dried berries, and still another was filled with seeds. "It's a little storehouse for the animals," Peter said. "Whenever I come back, I find more of the food has been eaten."

Niki sniffed at the nuts, but he was more interested in the feathers and droppings that lay on the floor. Peter was trying to put back a drawer that had stuck when he heard something that sent chills down his back.

"A-ooooo, A-ooooo." Somewhere in the freezing forest night wolves were calling.

Peter turned back to the drawer and shoved hard. It still didn't work. He started to shove with all his strength when Niki ran from his side to look through the door. Peter followed the fox's gaze. Silently moving through the blue-shadowed snow were six dark shapes.

Wolves!

Peter's heart beat wildly. In the fast-fading light he saw the wolves' yellow eyes staring up at him. He saw their cunning faces and their tongues hanging from their mouths.

Peter swallowed. What was he to do? How could he call for help? Already the night had become bitterly cold, and he knew he would freeze if he stayed too long in the tree house. He must get home quickly—but how?

From somewhere came the fearful calling of another wolf pack, their voices clear in the still, freezing air. "A-ooooo."

The wolves below became more excited. They pawed the snow, and the biggest lurched at the tree as if he wanted to climb it. He jumped once. He jumped again. He jumped still higher, and Peter saw a strange-looking paw.

It was Three-Toes!

Peter could see his cruel gray face and his white teeth flashing in the darkness—and he felt weak with fear. He reached for Niki, who had stayed close to him. He put his arm around the fox's warm body. For a second Niki allowed Peter to hold him, but then, suddenly, he shook himself free.

Before Peter knew what was happening, the fox jumped through the door and down into the snow!

There was a furious scramble of flashing white fangs and long gray bodies, and then—madly racing after their prey—the wolves dashed after Niki.

Peter climbed down the tree and ran as fast as he could. Somehow, even in the darkness, he found his way. Panting for breath, he arrived home just as his parents were getting ready to look for him. After he had told them what had happened, he said, "Have... you seen Niki?"

"No."

Peter said nothing but went to the stove. Never had the fire seemed so warm, but Peter did not look at the burning embers tonight because he did not want to see the animal faces. He couldn't stop thinking of the horrible dark shapes that had growled and leaped at him under the tree. Somewhere, out in the dark forest night, Niki was racing for his life. Was he alive? Would he ever come back?

Peter tasted salt in the corners of his mouth and knew he was crying. He longed to see the snow fox again. Peter's father put his arm around his shoulders and said, "It is hard to believe. Who would ever think that a fox would save a boy's life? What a mystery!"

But was it a mystery? Peter knew that Niki was far more intelligent than

anyone realized. Niki was... but suddenly Peter heard a sound at the door.

He listened carefully. Something was scratching outside. Peter jumped up. He ran to the front door, then to the back.

There, in the blue-shadowed snow, was Niki!

Kneeling down, Peter hugged the snow fox in his arms. He felt Niki's beating heart and his soft white fur brushed with ice crystals. For a long moment Niki buried his cold nose in Peter's neck. He licked the boy's cheek, but then he shook himself free and jumped from Peter's arms. He moved silently across the snow and into the forest.

The Author-Artist

ARNOLD DOBRIN says he is a "compulsive traveler." And, indeed, he has traveled widely—in the United States, in Asia, and in Europe. For two years the Dobrins lived in Rome, Italy, where he painted "in the most romantic studio in the world which looked out over the tile roofs and church domes of Trastevere, one of the oldest sections of the city."

Arnold Dobrin was born in Omaha, Nebraska, but most of his life, when he has not been traveling, has been spent in California. He presently lives in Connecticut with his wife, Norma, and their two sons.

Mr. Dobrin is the author of *Little Monk and the Tiger: A Tale of Thailand*, *Taro and the Sea Turtles: A Tale of Japan*, and *Carmello's Cat: The Story of a Roman Christmas*.